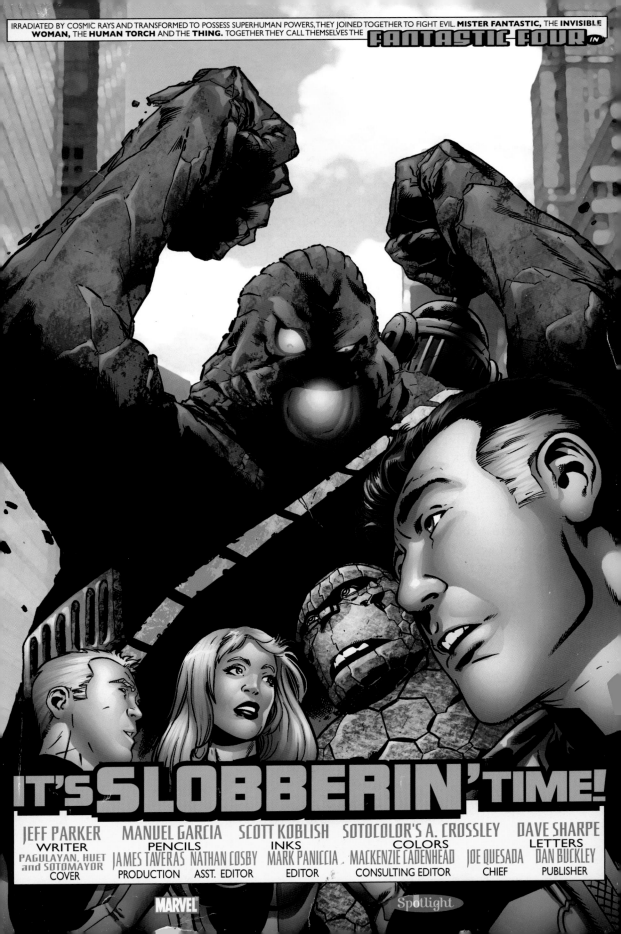

IRRADIATED BY COSMIC RAYS AND TRANSFORMED TO POSSESS SUPERHUMAN POWERS, THEY JOINED TOGETHER TO FIGHT EVIL. **MISTER FANTASTIC**, THE **INVISIBLE WOMAN**, THE **HUMAN TORCH** AND THE **THING**. TOGETHER THEY CALL THEMSELVES THE **FANTASTIC FOUR** *IN*

IT'S SLOBBERIN' TIME!

JEFF PARKER
WRITER
PAGULAYAN, HUET
and SOTOMAYOR
COVER

MANUEL GARCIA
PENCILS
JAMES TAVERAS
PRODUCTION

SCOTT KOBLISH
INKS
NATHAN COSBY
ASST. EDITOR

SOTOCOLOR'S A. CROSSLEY
COLORS
MARK PANICCIA
EDITOR

DAVE SHARPE
LETTERS
MACKENZIE CADENHEAD
CONSULTING EDITOR

JOE QUESADA
CHIEF

DAN BUCKLEY
PUBLISHER

MARVEL

Spotlight

VISIT US AT
www.abdopublishing.com

Spotlight library bound edition © 2007. Spotlight is a division of ABDO Publishing
Company, Edina, Minnesota.

Cataloging Data

Parker, Jeff
    Fantastic Four in it's slobberin' time! / Jeff Parker, writer ; Manuel Garcia, pen-
cils ; Scott Koblish, inks. -- Library bound ed.
        p. cm. -- (Fantastic Four)
    Summary: Irradiated by cosmic rays and transformed to possess superhuman
powers, Mr. Fantastic, the Invisible Woman, the Human Torch, and the Thing join
together to fight evil.
    "Marvel age"--Cover.
    Revision of the March 2006 issue of Marvel adventures Fantastic Four.
    ISBN-13: 978-1-59961-202-7
    ISBN-10: 1-59961-202-X
    1. Fantastic Four (Fictitious characters)--Comic books, strips, etc.--Fiction. 2.
Graphic novels. I. Title. II. Title: It's slobberin' time! III. Series.

    741.5dc22

All Spotlight books are reinforced library binding
and manufactured in the United States of America

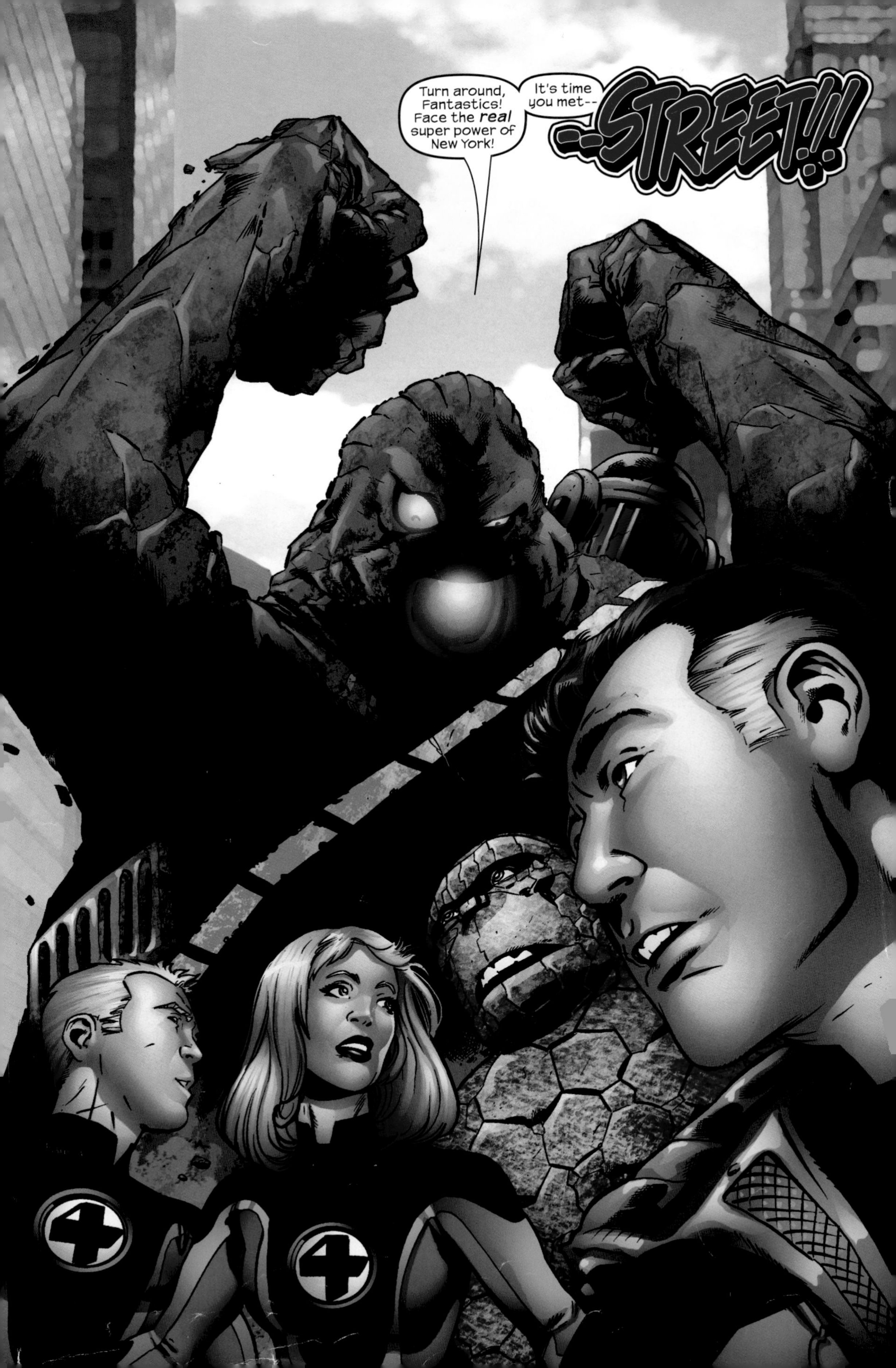
Turn around, Fantastics! Face the *real* super power of New York!
It's time you met--
--STREET!!!

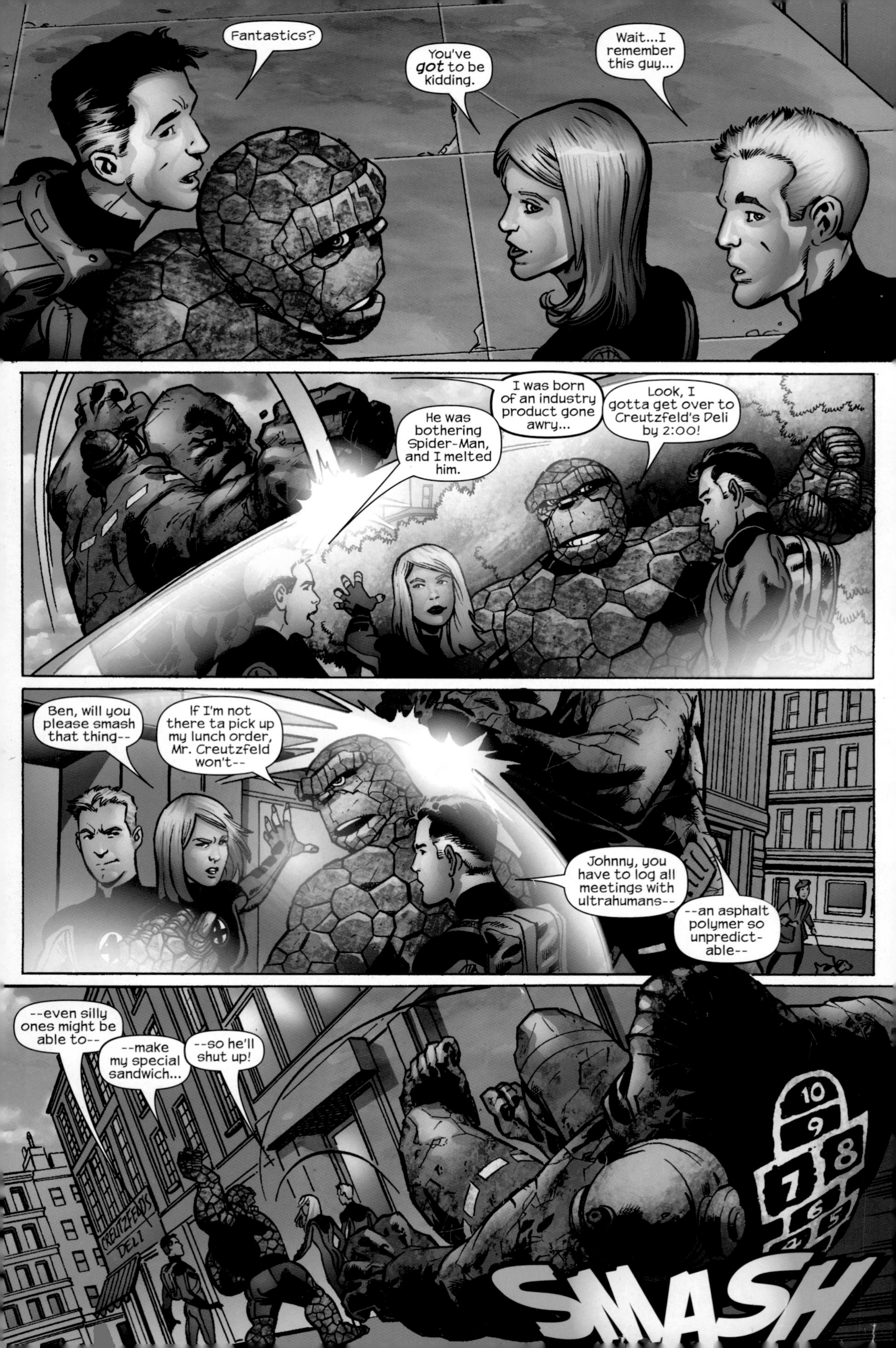
Fantastics?
You've got to be kidding.
Wait...I remember this guy...
He was bothering Spider-Man, and I melted him.
I was born of an industry product gone awry...
Look, I gotta get over to Creutzfeld's Deli by 2:00!
Ben, will you please smash that thing--
If I'm not there ta pick up my lunch order, Mr. Creutzfeld won't--
Johnny, you have to log all meetings with ultrahumans--
--an asphalt polymer so unpredict-able--
--even silly ones might be able to--
--make my special sandwich...
--so he'll shut up!
CREUTZFELD'S DELI
10
9
8
7
6
5
SMASH

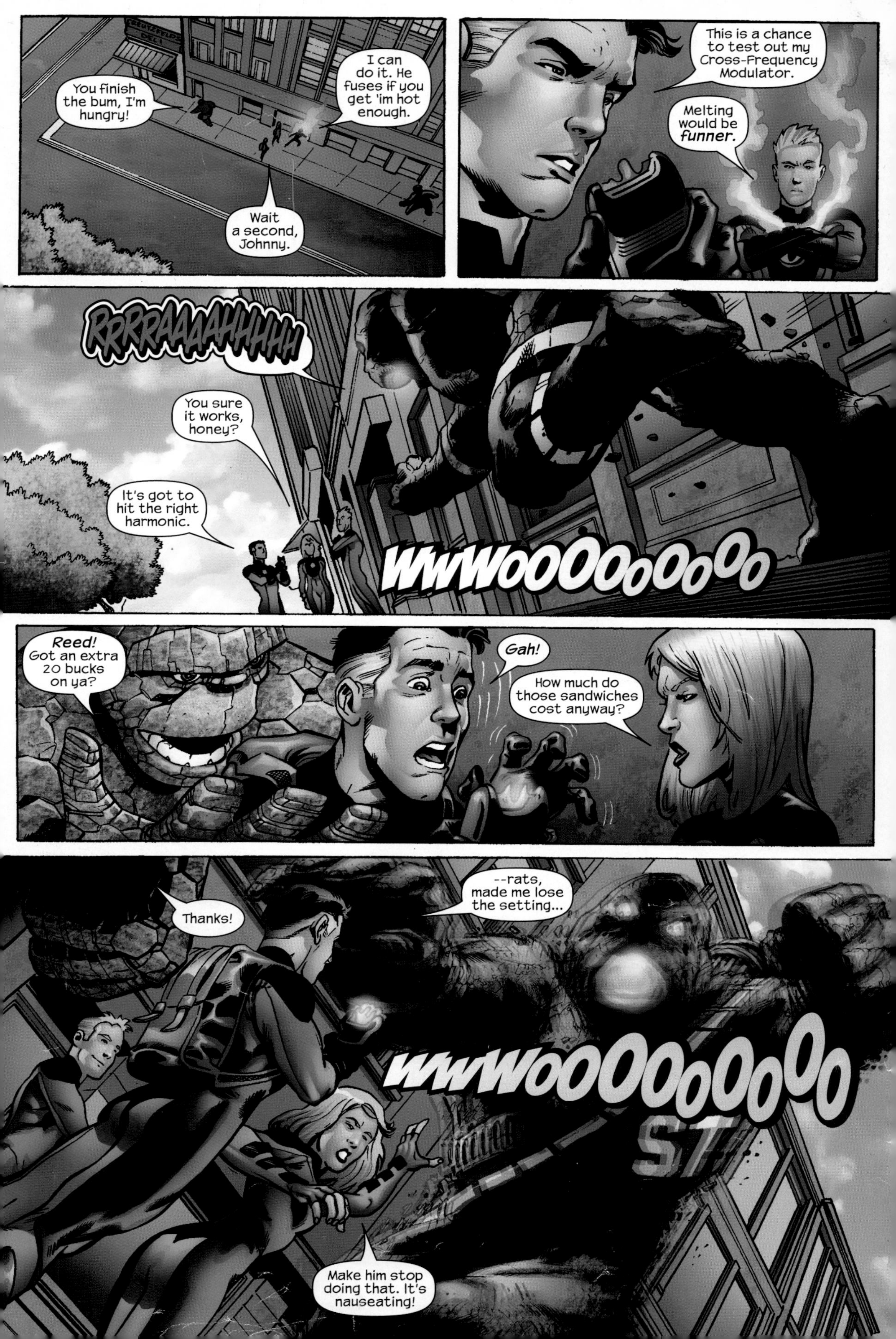

You finish the bum, I'm hungry!
I can do it. He fuses if you get 'im hot enough.
Wait a second, Johnny.
This is a chance to test out my Cross-Frequency Modulator.
Melting would be *funner.*
RRRRAAAAHHHHH
You sure it works, honey?
It's got to hit the right harmonic.
WWWOOOOOOOOO
Reed! Got an extra 20 bucks on ya?
Gah!
How much do those sandwiches cost anyway?
Thanks!
--rats, made me lose the setting...
WWWOOOOOOOOOOOO
Make him stop doing that. It's nauseating!

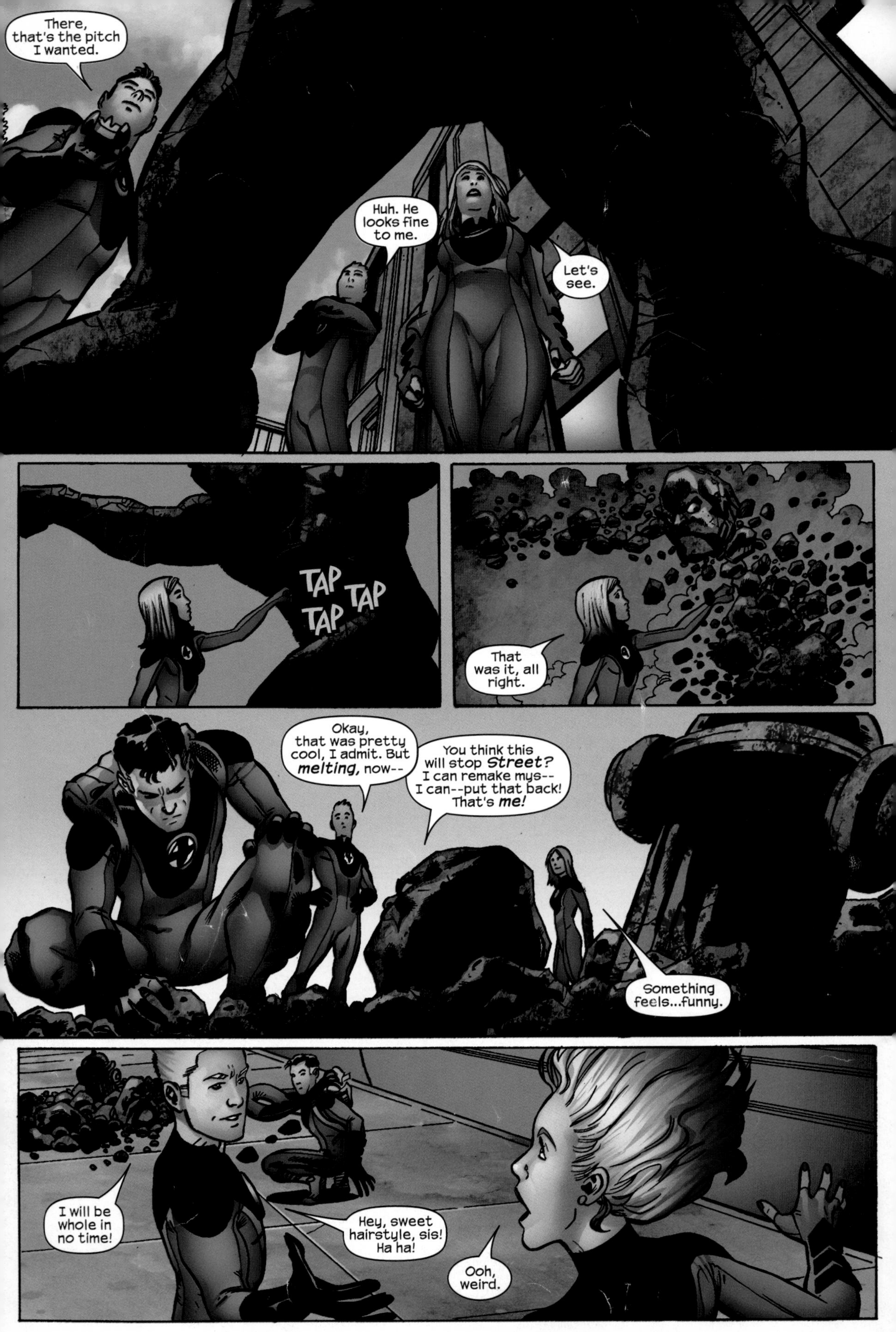
There, that's the pitch I wanted.
Huh. He looks fine to me.
Let's see.
TAP TAP TAP
That was it, all right.
Okay, that was pretty cool, I admit. But *melting,* now--
You think this will stop *Street?* I can remake mys-- I can--put that back! That's *me!*
Something feels...funny.
I will be whole in no time!
Hey, sweet hairstyle, sis! Ha ha!
Ooh, weird.

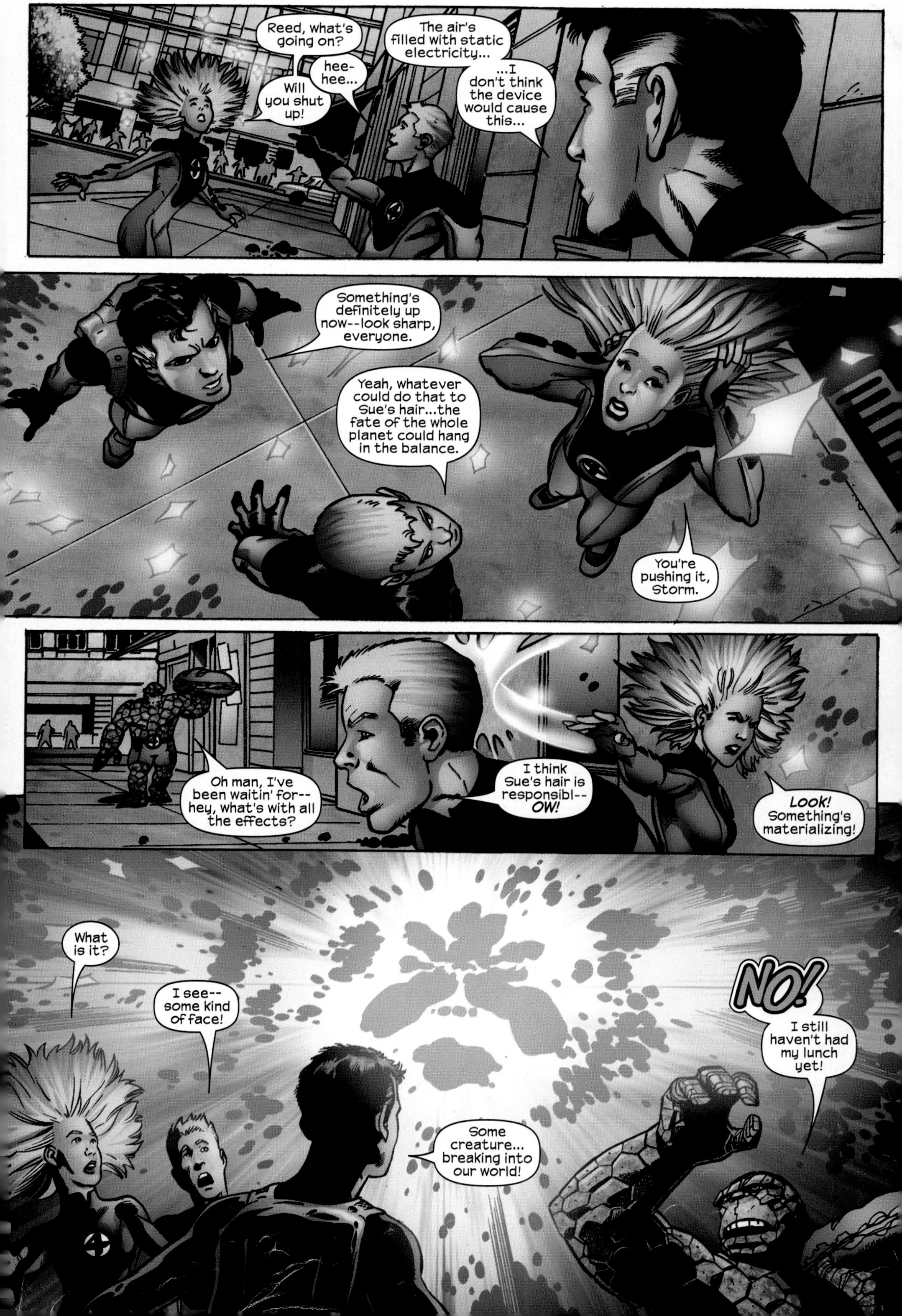

Reed, what's going on?
Will you shut up!
hee-hee...
The air's filled with static electricity...
...I don't think the device would cause this...
Something's definitely up now--look sharp, everyone.
Yeah, whatever could do that to Sue's hair...the fate of the whole planet could hang in the balance.
You're pushing it, Storm.
Oh man, I've been waitin' for--hey, what's with all the effects?
I think Sue's hair is responsibl--OW!
LOOK! Something's materializing!
What is it?
I see--some kind of face!
Some creature... breaking into our world!
NO!
I still haven't had my lunch yet!

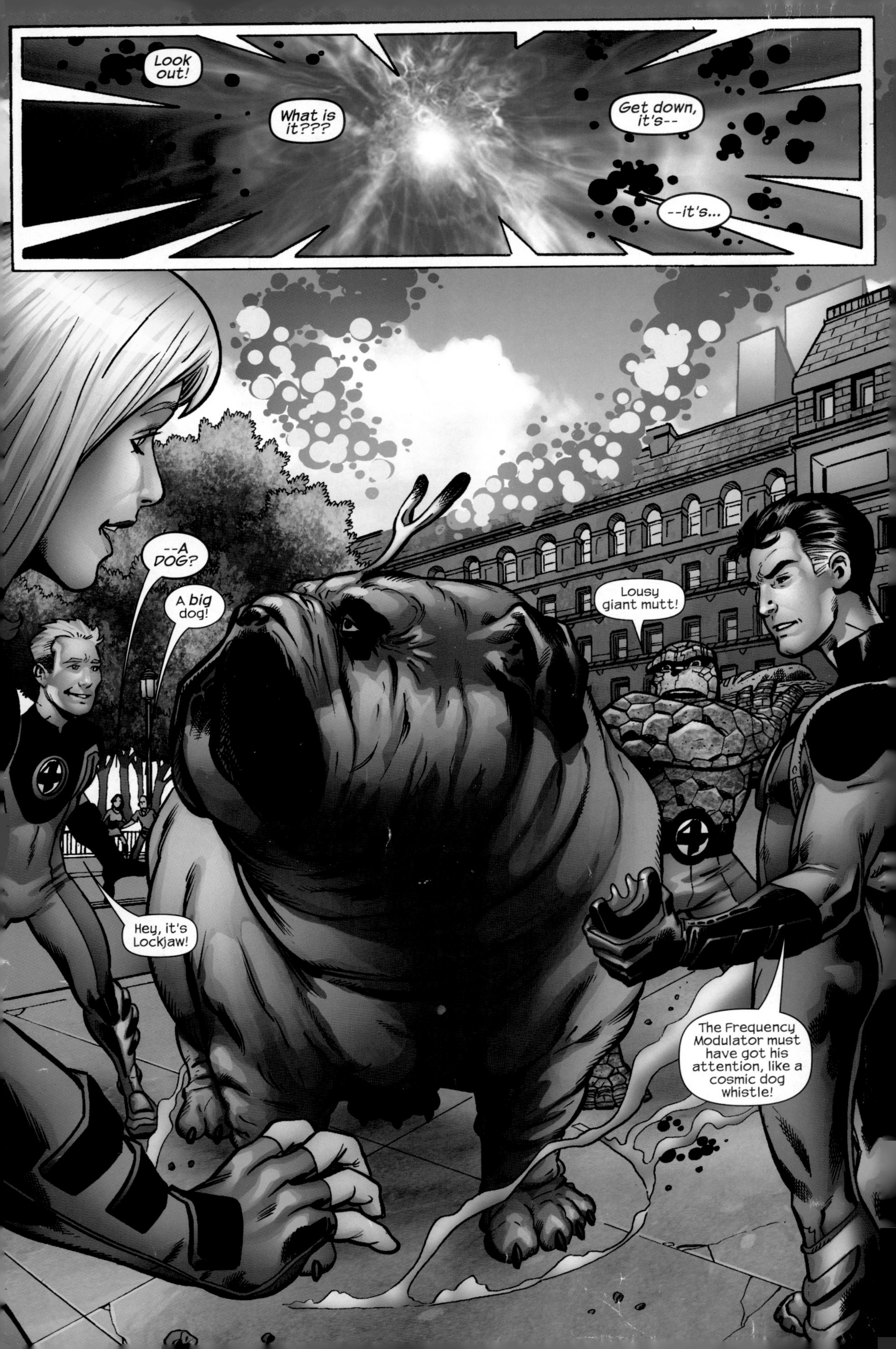
Look out!
What is it???
Get down, it's--
--it's...
--A DOG?
A big dog!
Hey, it's Lockjaw!
Lousy giant mutt!
The Frequency Modulator must have got his attention, like a cosmic dog whistle!

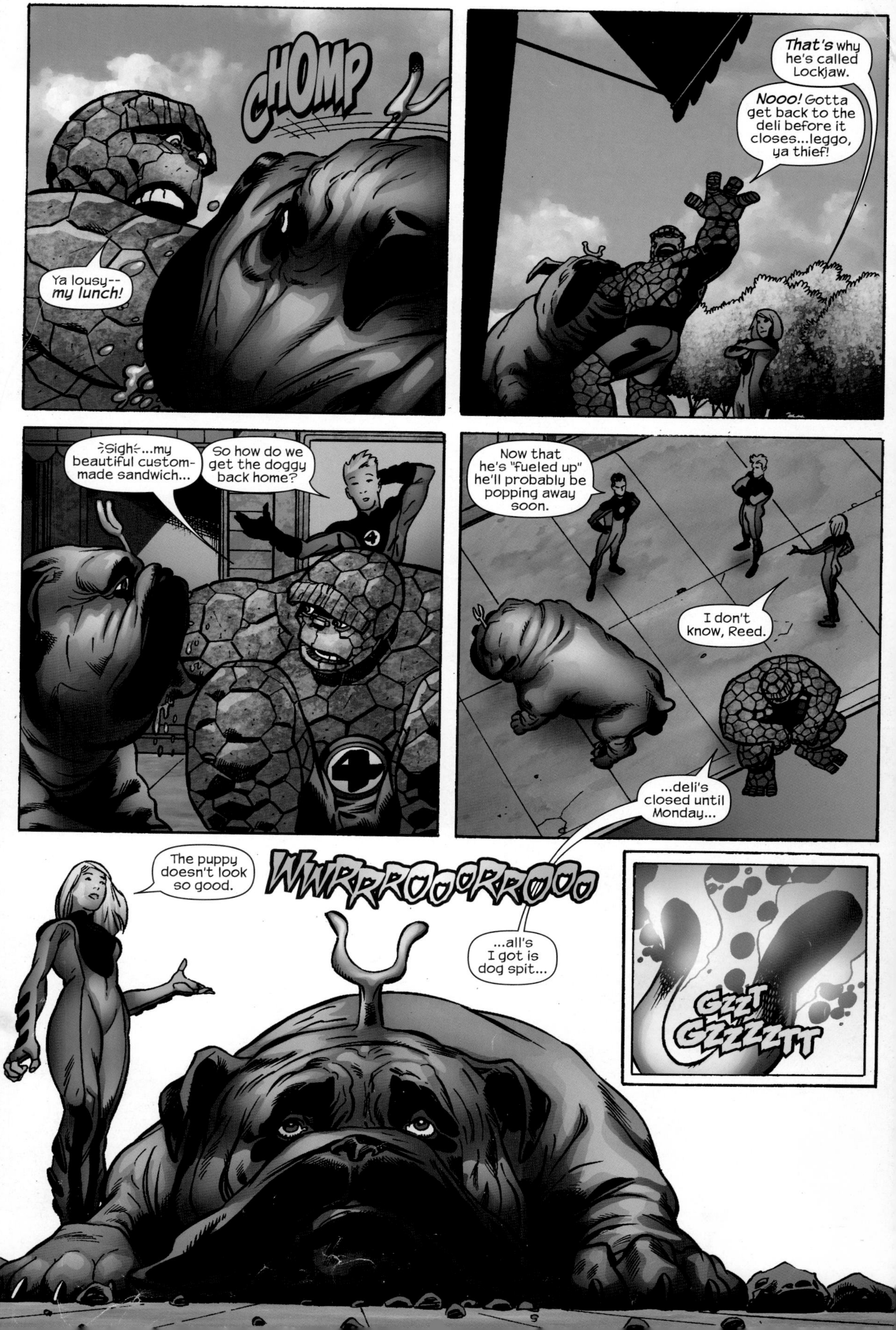
CHOMP
Ya lousy-- my lunch!
That's why he's called Lockjaw.
Nooo! Gotta get back to the deli before it closes...leggo, ya thief!
Sigh...my beautiful custom-made sandwich...
So how do we get the doggy back home?
Now that he's "fueled up" he'll probably be popping away soon.
I don't know, Reed.
...deli's closed until Monday...
The puppy doesn't look so good.
WWRRROOORRROOO
...all's I got is dog spit...
GZZT GZZZZTT

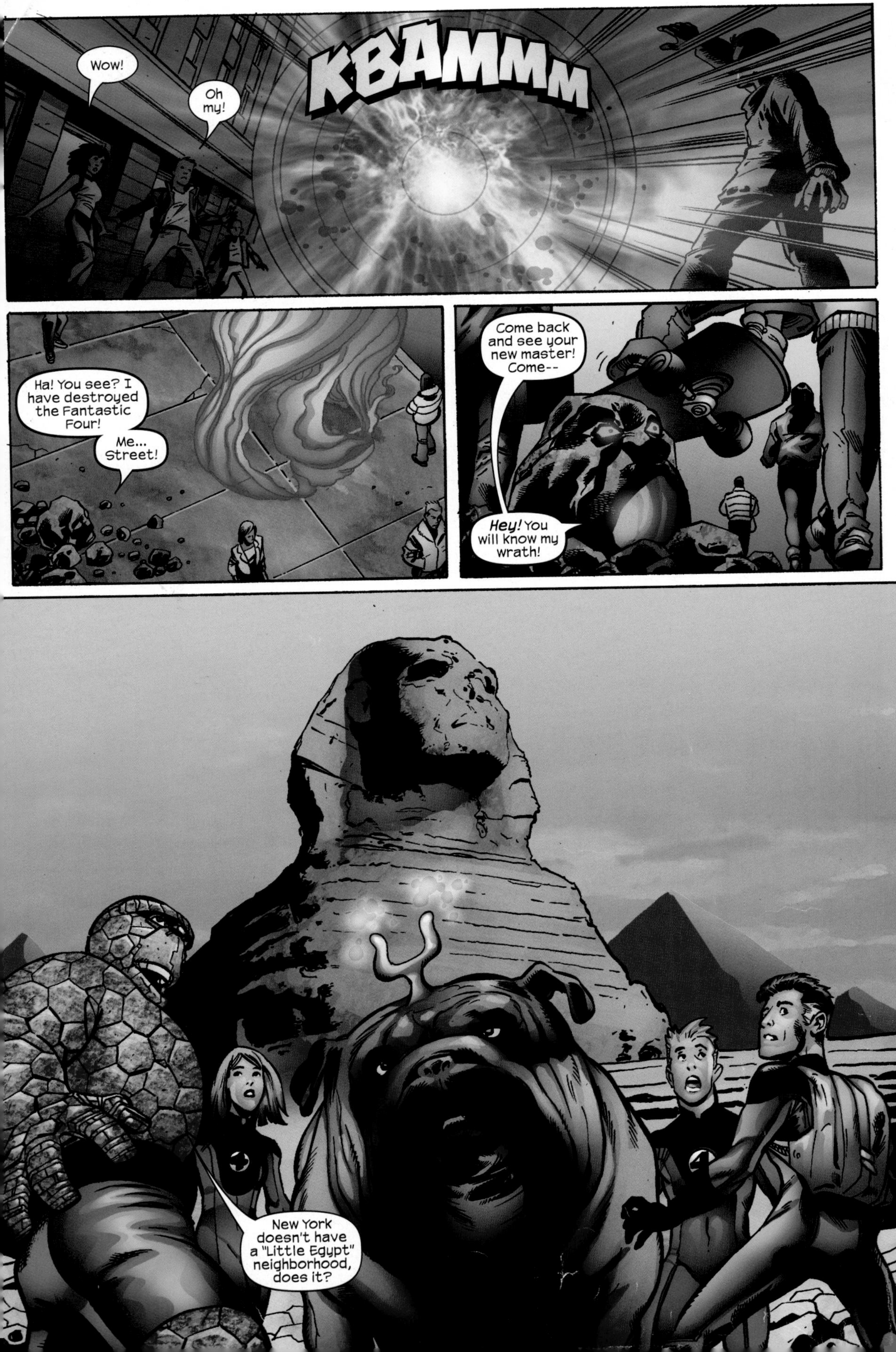
Wow!
Oh my!
KBAMMM
Ha! You see? I have destroyed the Fantastic Four!
Me... Street!
Come back and see your new master! Come--
Hey! You will know my wrath!
New York doesn't have a "Little Egypt" neighborhood, does it?

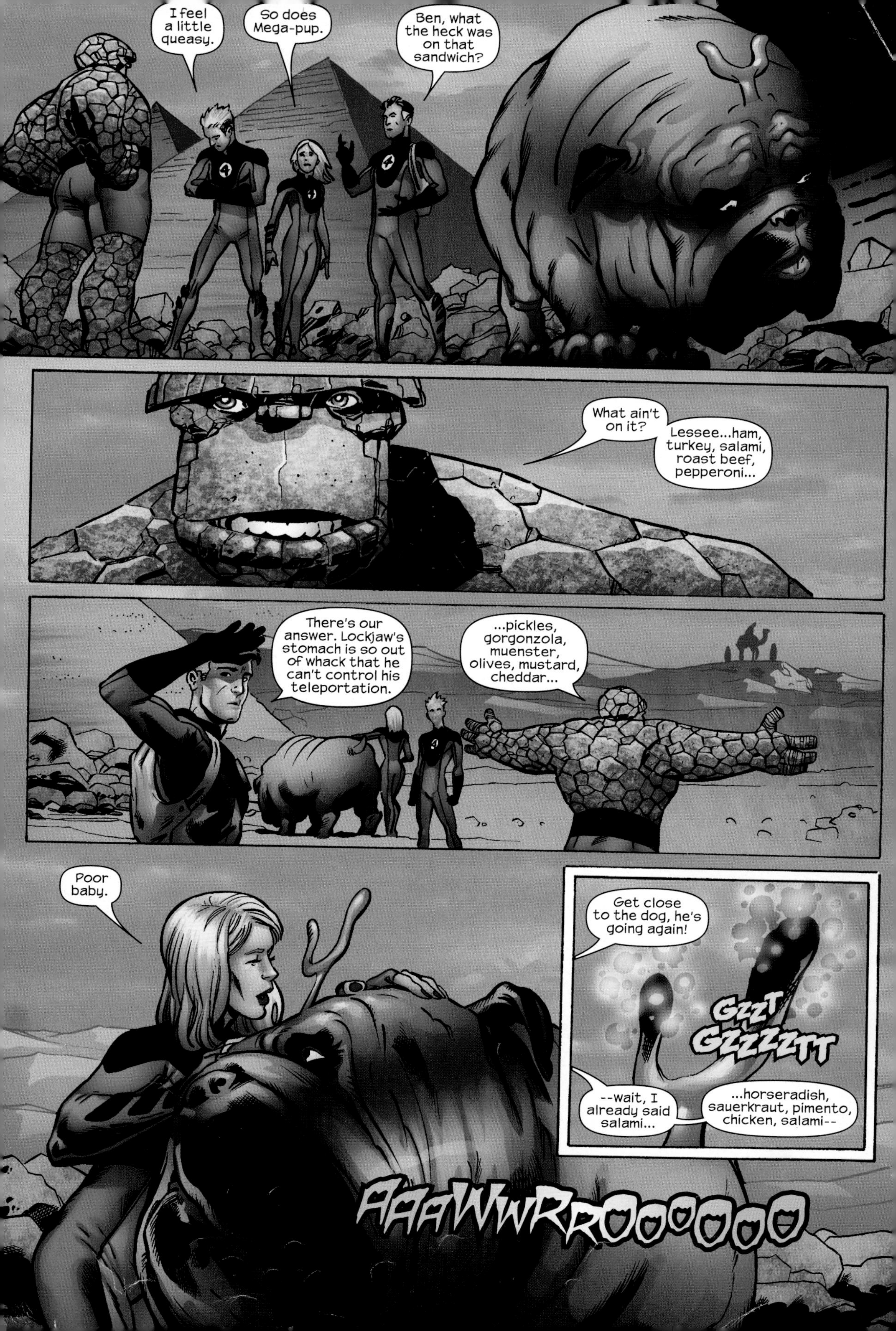
I feel a little queasy.
So does Mega-pup.
Ben, what the heck was on that sandwich?
What ain't on it?
Lessee...ham, turkey, salami, roast beef, pepperoni...
There's our answer. Lockjaw's stomach is so out of whack that he can't control his teleportation.
...pickles, gorgonzola, muenster, olives, mustard, cheddar...
Poor baby.
Get close to the dog, he's going again!
GZZT GZZZZZTT
--wait, I already said salami...
...horseradish, sauerkraut, pimento, chicken, salami--
AAAWWRROOOOOOO

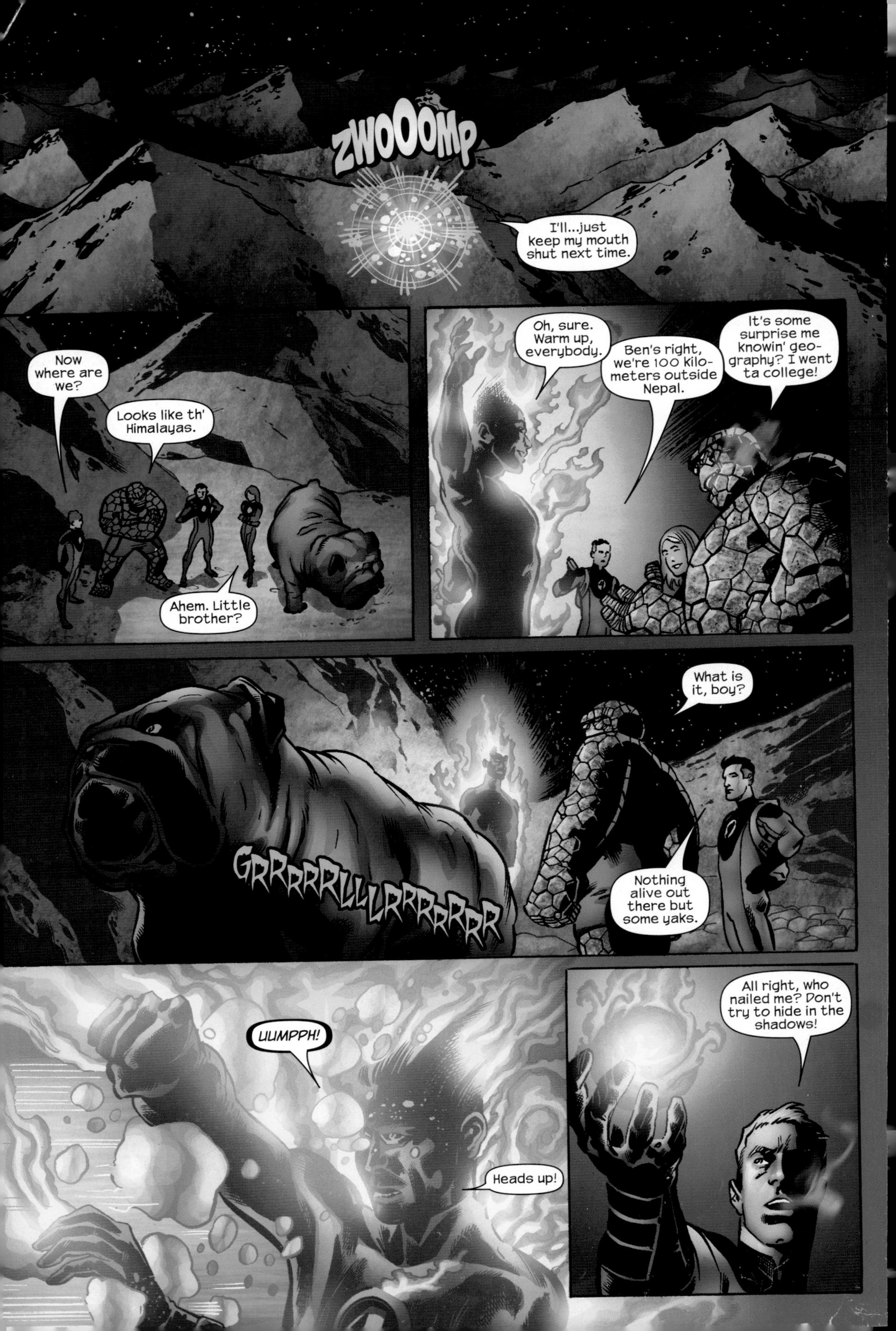
ZWOOOMP
I'll...just keep my mouth shut next time.
Now where are we?
Looks like th' Himalayas.
Ahem. Little brother?
Oh, sure. Warm up, everybody.
Ben's right, we're 100 kilometers outside Nepal.
It's some surprise me knowin' geography? I went ta college!
GRRRRRLLLRRRRRRR
What is it, boy?
Nothing alive out there but some yaks.
UUMPPH!
Heads up!
All right, who nailed me? Don't try to hide in the shadows!

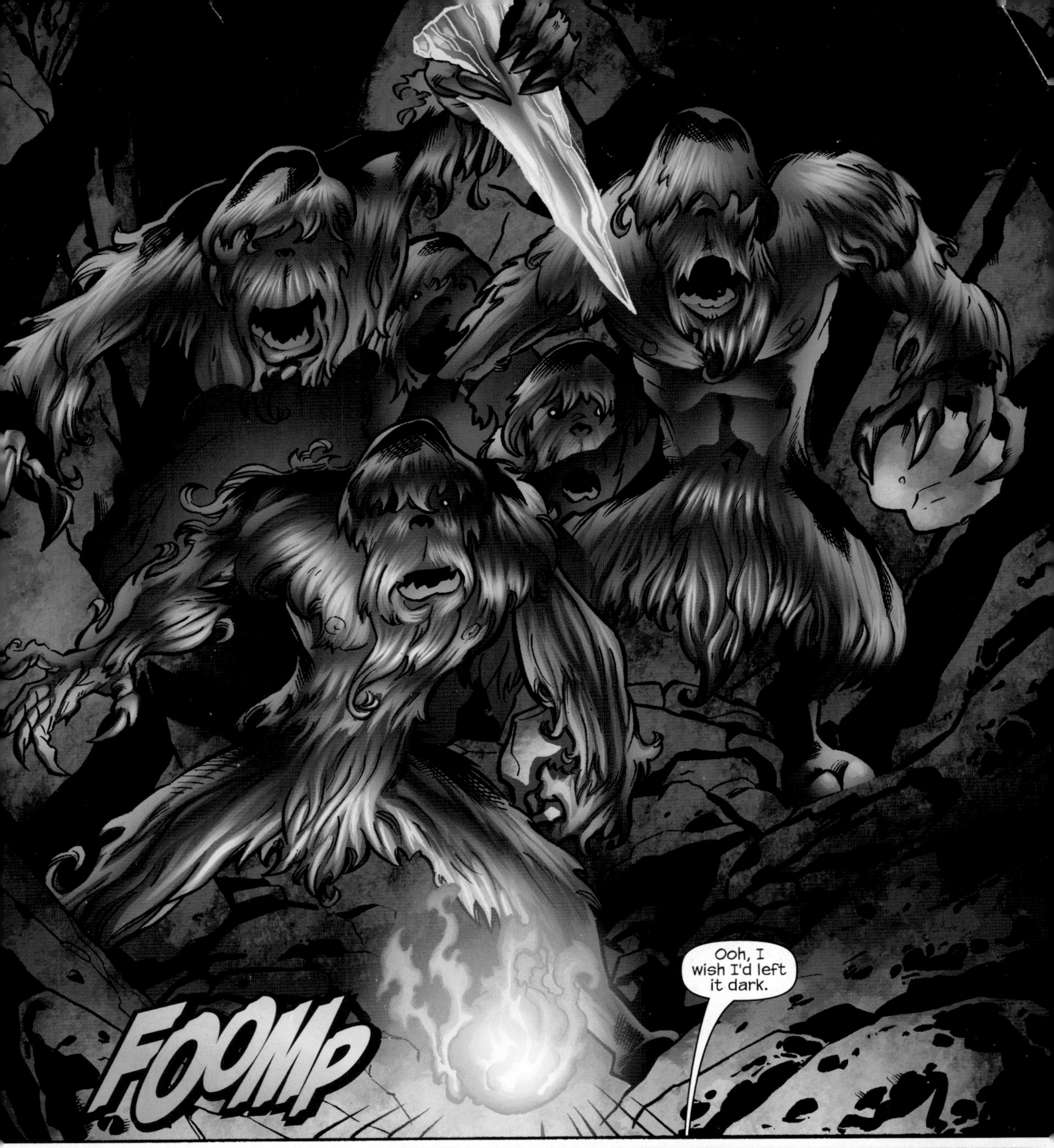
FOOMP
Ooh, I wish I'd left it dark.

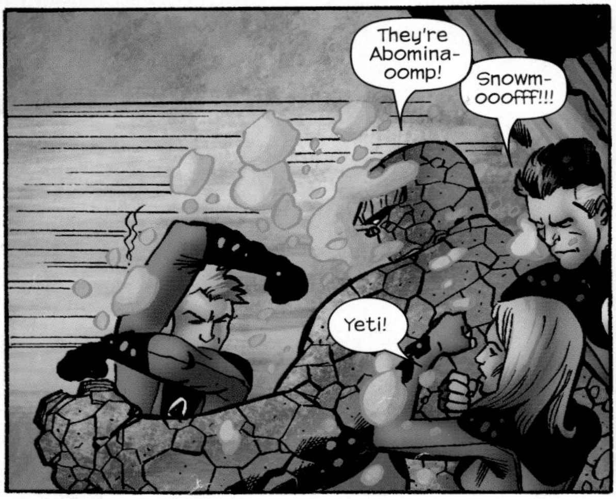
They're Abomina-oomp!
Snowm-ooofff!!!
Yeti!

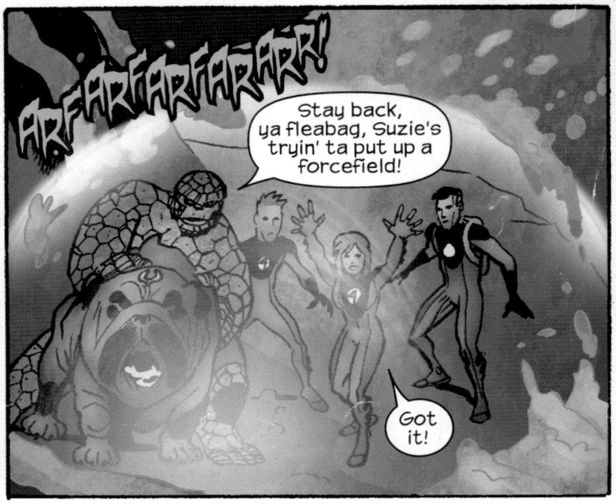
ARFARFARFARFARRR!
Stay back, ya fleabag, Suzie's tryin' ta put up a forcefield!
Got it!

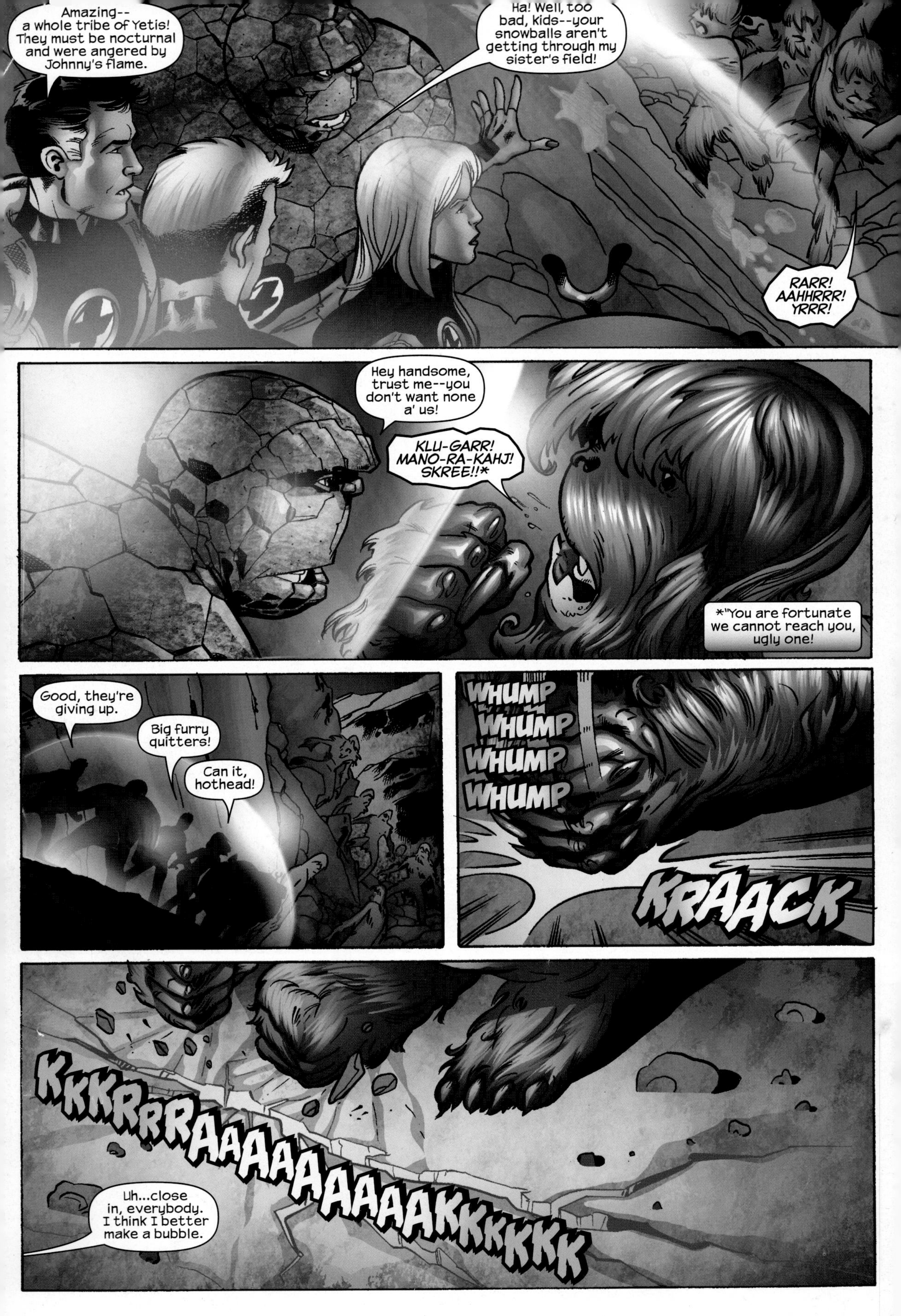

Amazing-- a whole tribe of Yetis! They must be nocturnal and were angered by Johnny's flame.
Ha! Well, too bad, kids--your snowballs aren't getting through my sister's field!
RARR! AAHHRRR! YRRR!
Hey handsome, trust me--you don't want none a' us!
KLU-GARR! MANO-RA-KAHJ! SKREE!!*
*"You are fortunate we cannot reach you, ugly one!
Good, they're giving up.
Big furry quitters!
Can it, hothead!
WHUMP
WHUMP
WHUMP
WHUMP
KRAACK
KKKRRRRAAAAAAAAAAKKKKKKK
Uh...close in, everybody. I think I better make a bubble.

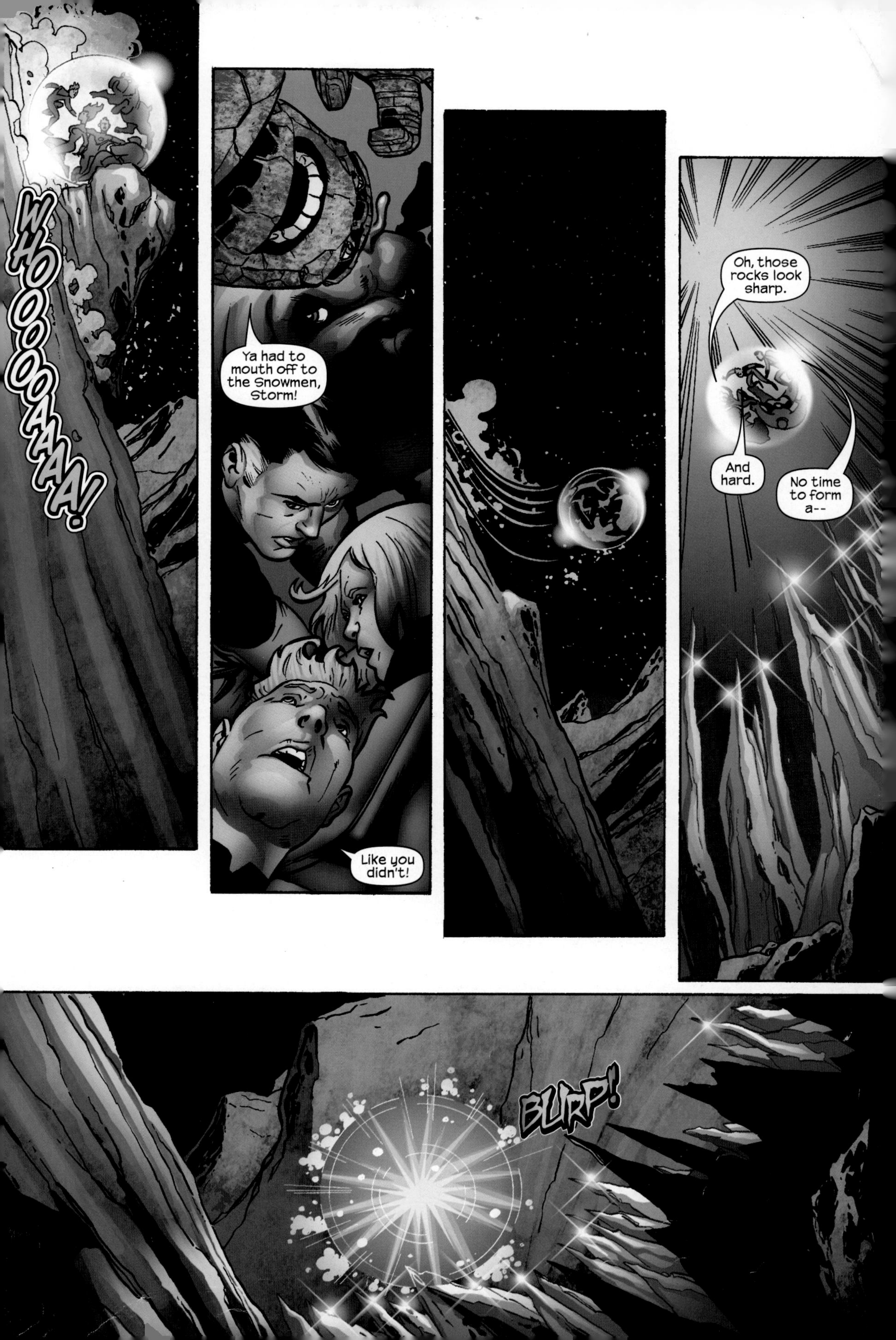
WHOOOOOAAAA!
Ya had to mouth off to the Snowmen, Storm!
Like you didn't!
Oh, those rocks look sharp.
And hard.
No time to form a--
BURP!

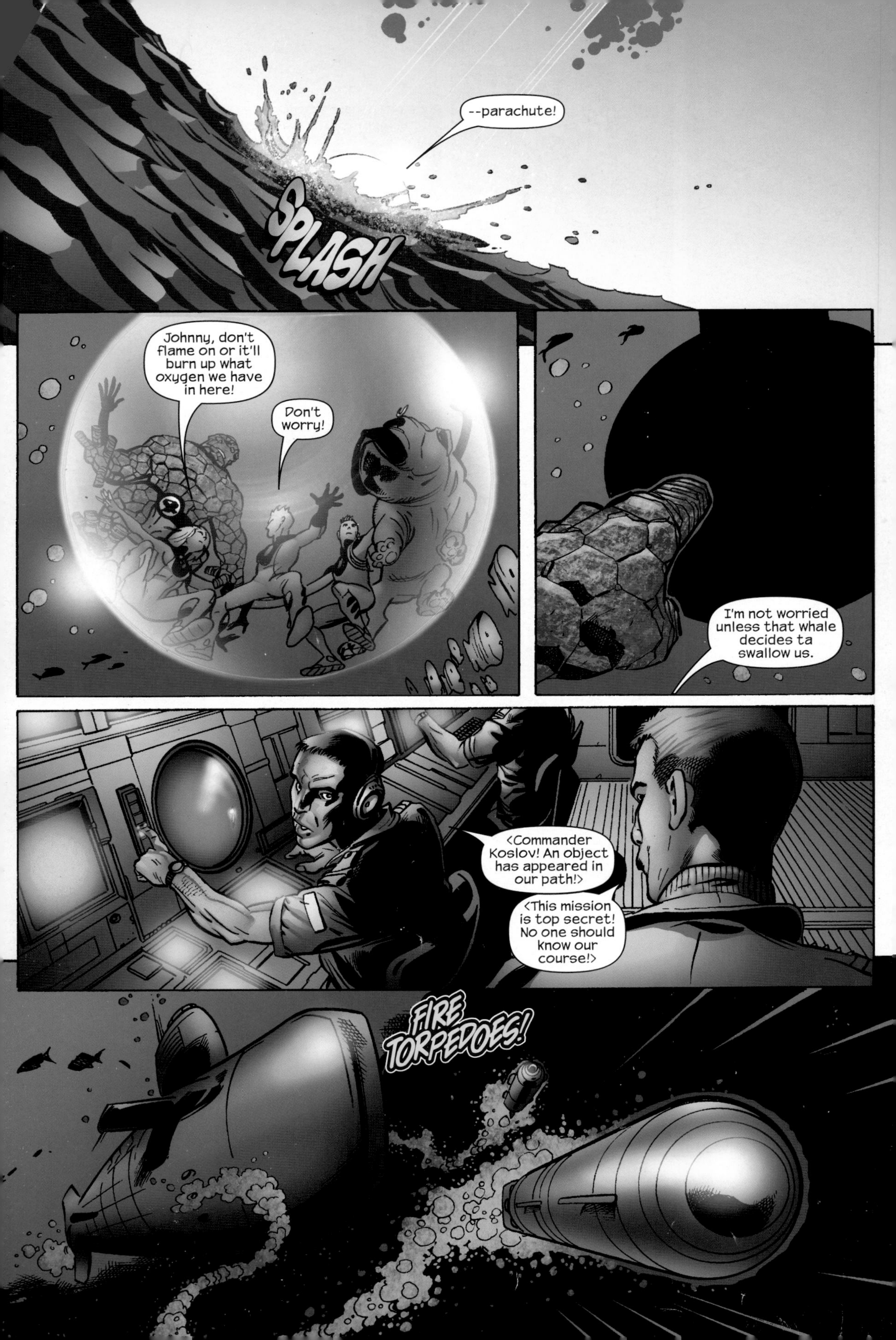
--parachute!
SPLASH
Johnny, don't flame on or it'll burn up what oxygen we have in here!
Don't worry!
I'm not worried unless that whale decides ta swallow us.
<Commander Koslov! An object has appeared in our path!>
<This mission is top secret! No one should know our course!>
FIRE TORPEDOES!

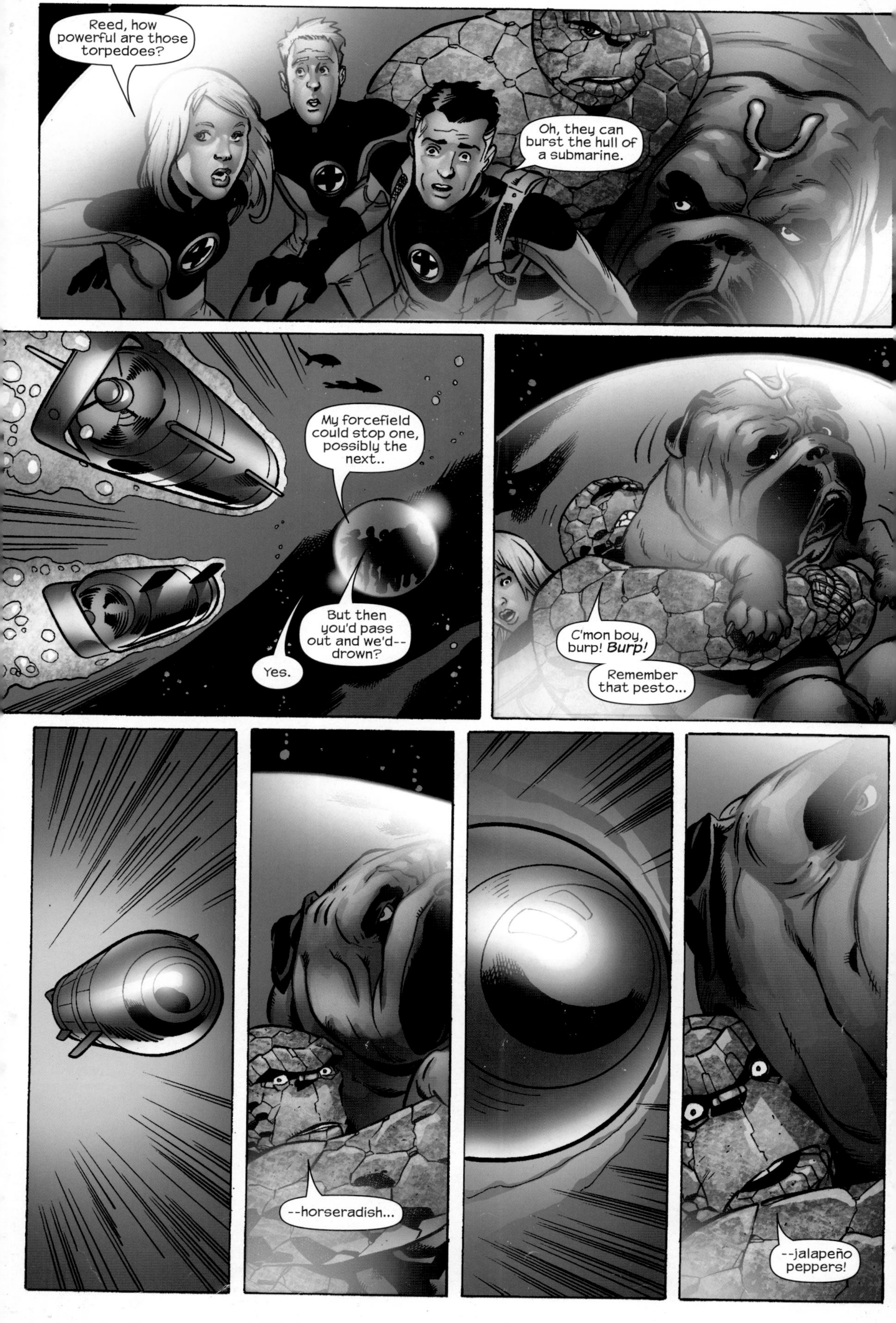
Reed, how powerful are those torpedoes?
Oh, they can burst the hull of a submarine.
My forcefield could stop one, possibly the next..
But then you'd pass out and we'd--drown?
Yes.
C'mon boy, burp! **Burp!**
Remember that pesto...
--horseradish...
--jalapeño peppers!

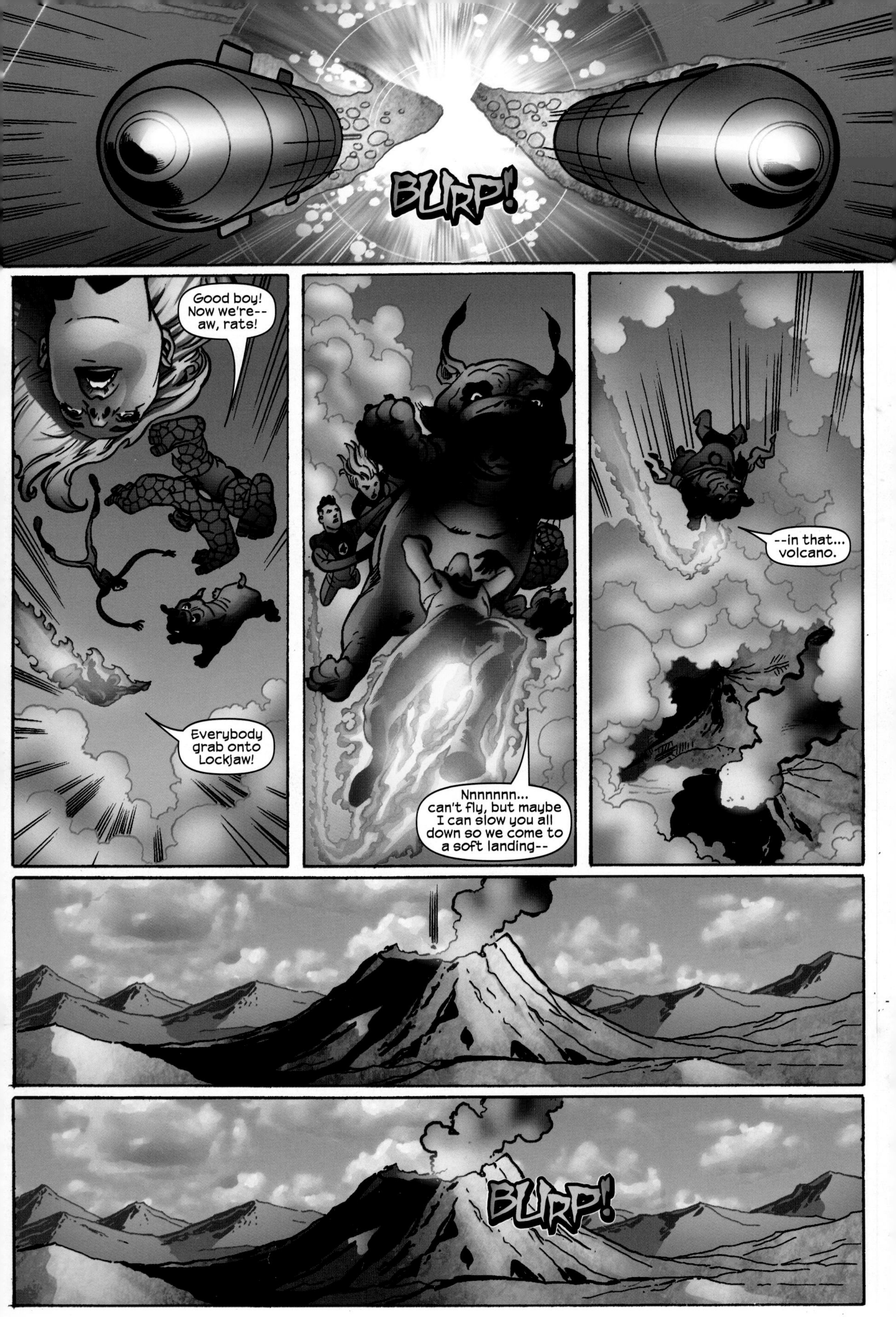
BURP!
Good boy! Now we're-- aw, rats!
Everybody grab onto Lockjaw!
Nnnnnnn... can't fly, but maybe I can slow you all down so we come to a soft landing--
--in that... volcano.
BURP!

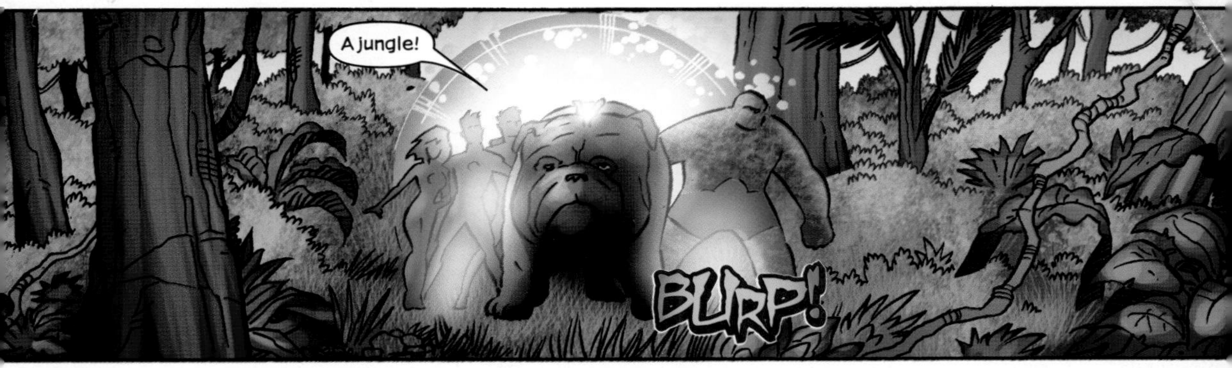
A jungle!
BURP!

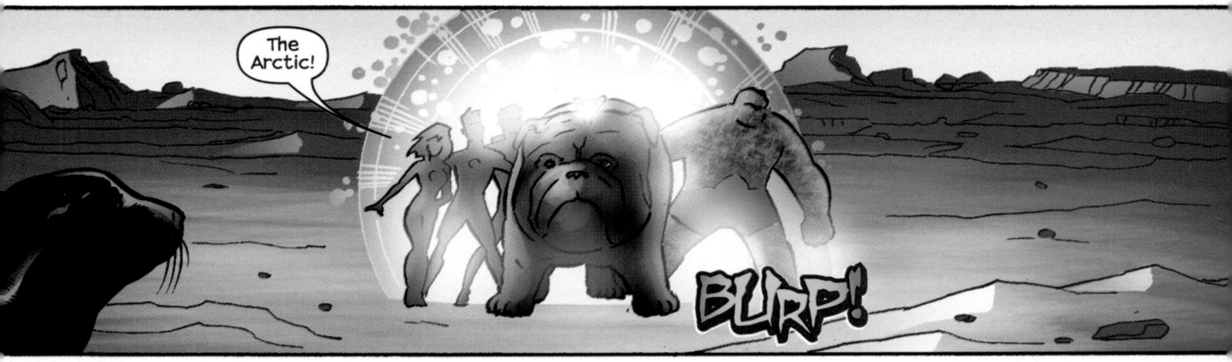
The Arctic!
BURP!

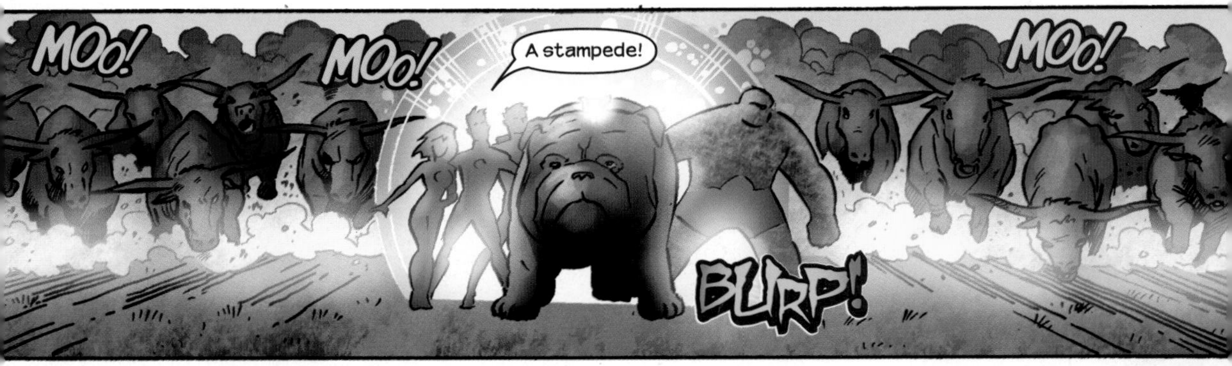
MOO!
MOO!
A stampede!
MOO!
BURP!

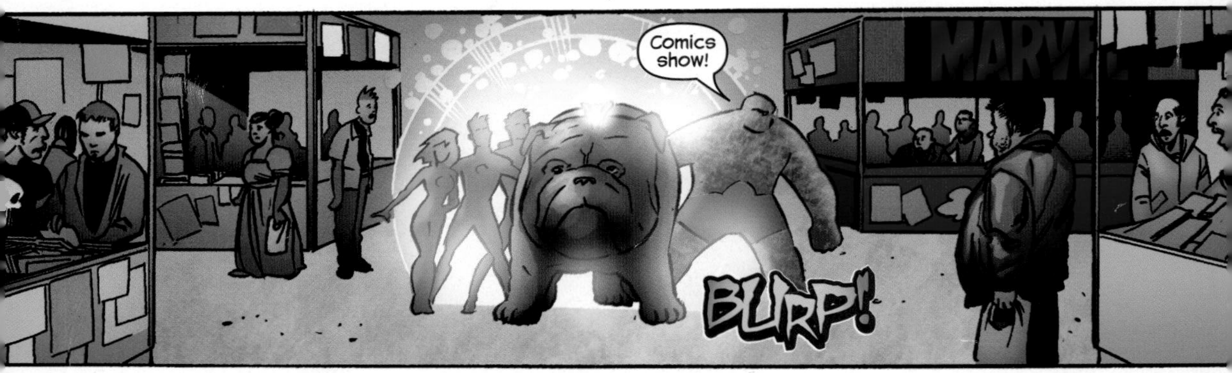
Comics show!
BURP!

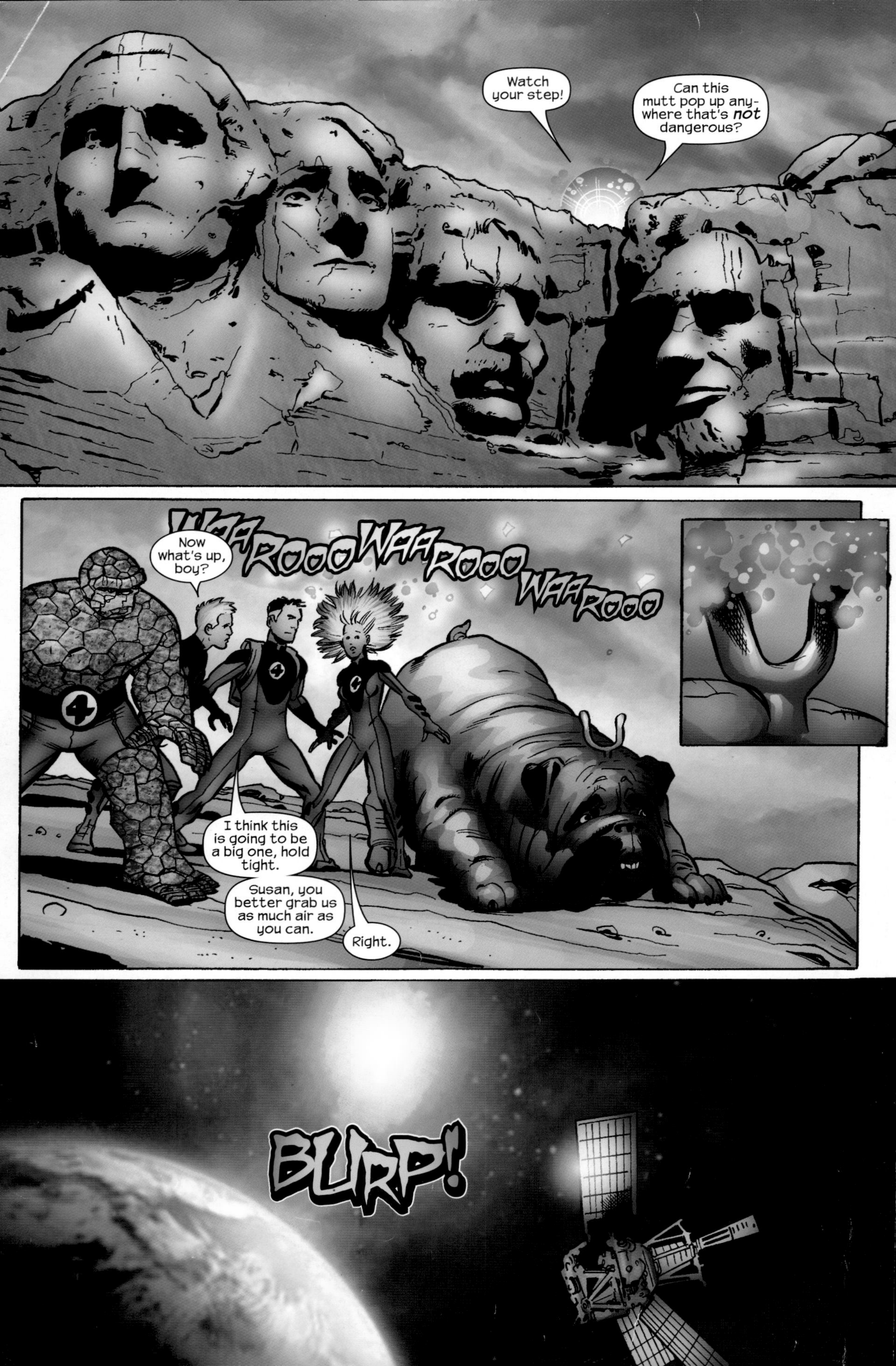
Watch your step!
Can this mutt pop up anywhere that's *not* dangerous?
WAAROOO WAAROOO WAAROOO
Now what's up, boy?
I think this is going to be a big one, hold tight.
Susan, you better grab us as much air as you can.
Right.
BURP!

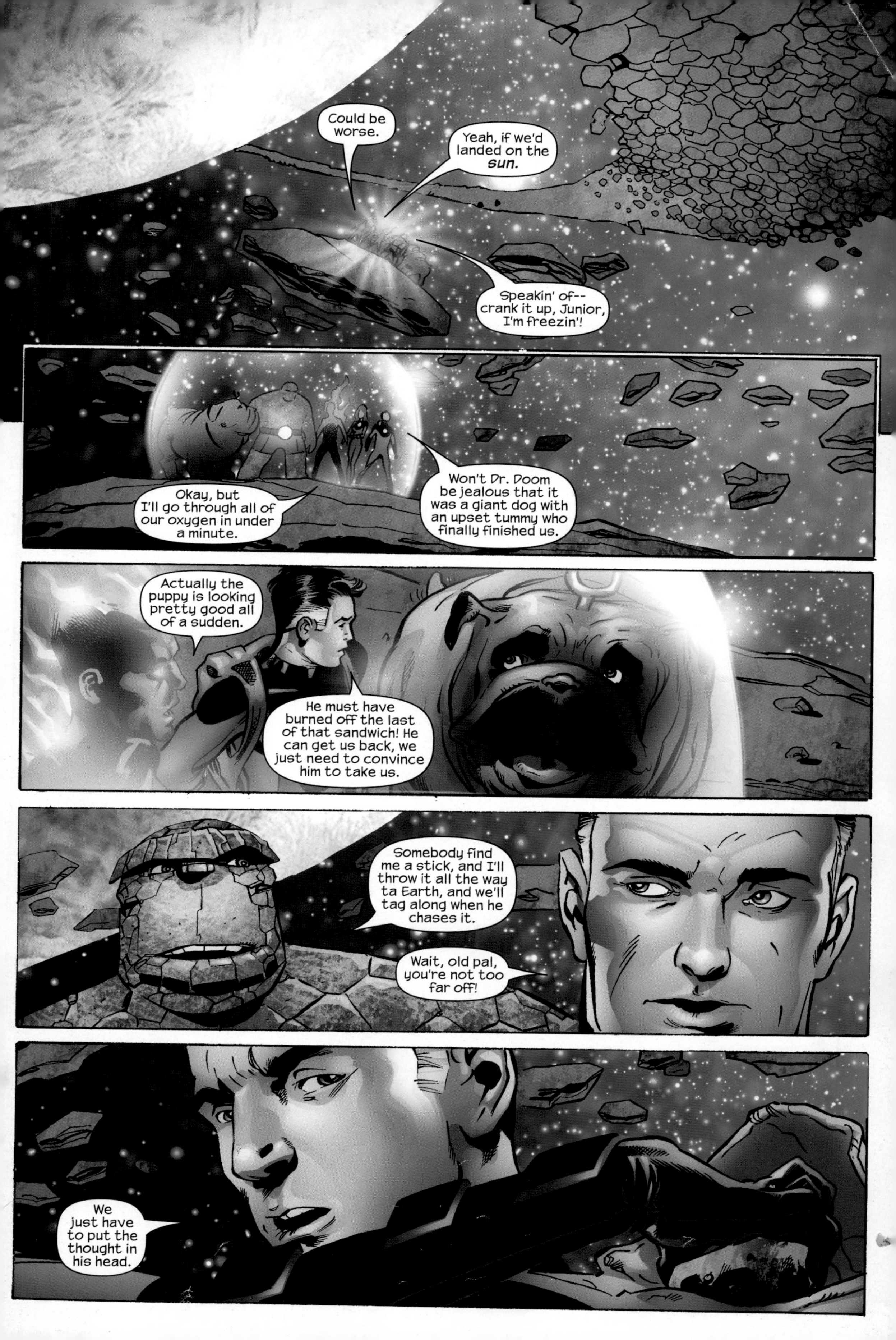

Could be worse.
Yeah, if we'd landed on the *sun.*
Speakin' of-- crank it up, Junior, I'm freezin'!
Okay, but I'll go through all of our oxygen in under a minute.
Won't Dr. Doom be jealous that it was a giant dog with an upset tummy who finally finished us.
Actually the puppy is looking pretty good all of a sudden.
He must have burned off the last of that sandwich! He can get us back, we just need to convince him to take us.
Somebody find me a stick, and I'll throw it all the way ta Earth, and we'll tag along when he chases it.
Wait, old pal, you're not too far off!
We just have to put the thought in his head.

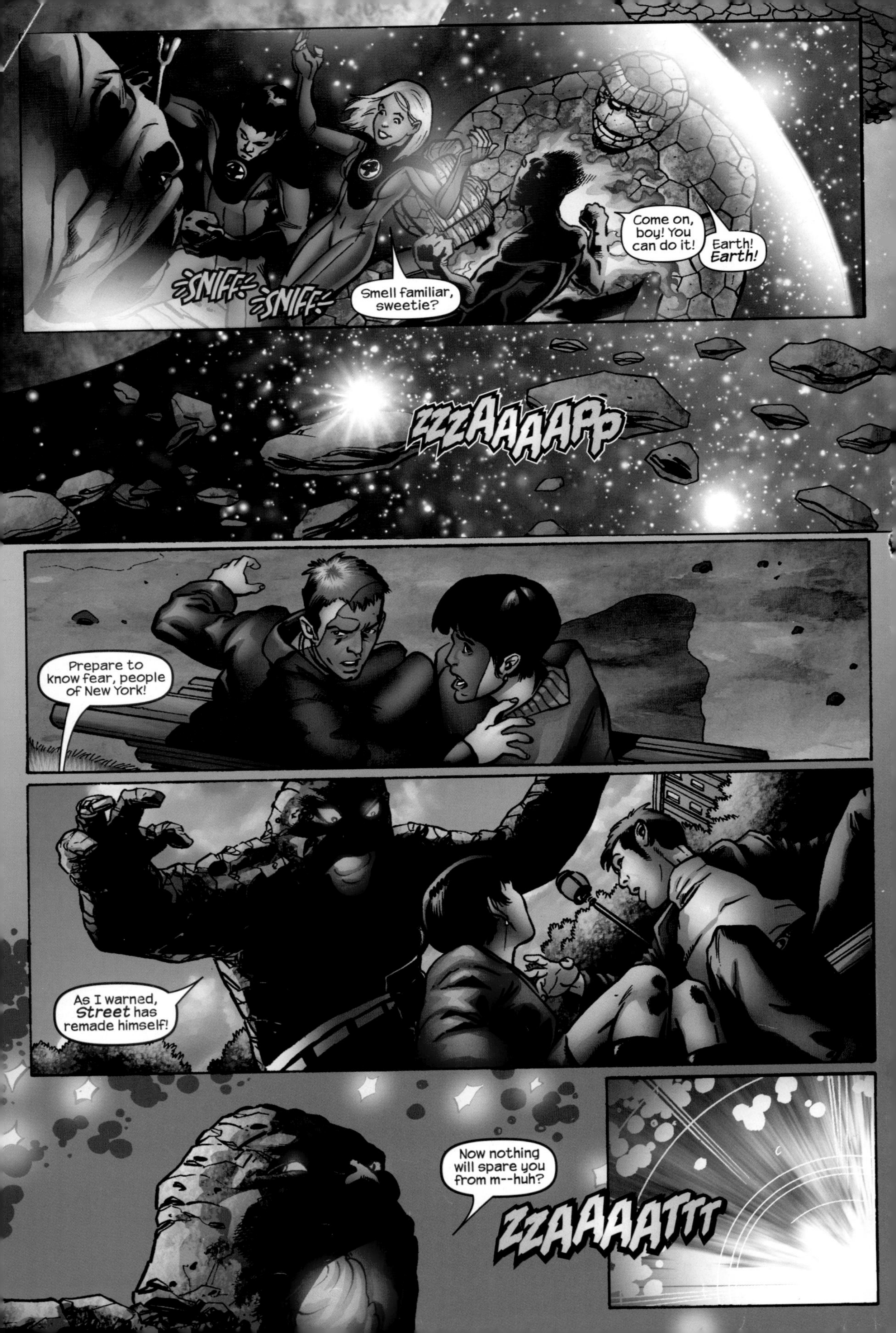
SNIFF
SNIFF
Smell familiar, sweetie?
Come on, boy! You can do it!
Earth! Earth!
ZZZAAAAPP
Prepare to know fear, people of New York!
As I warned, Street has remade himself!
Now nothing will spare you from m--huh?
ZZAAAATTT

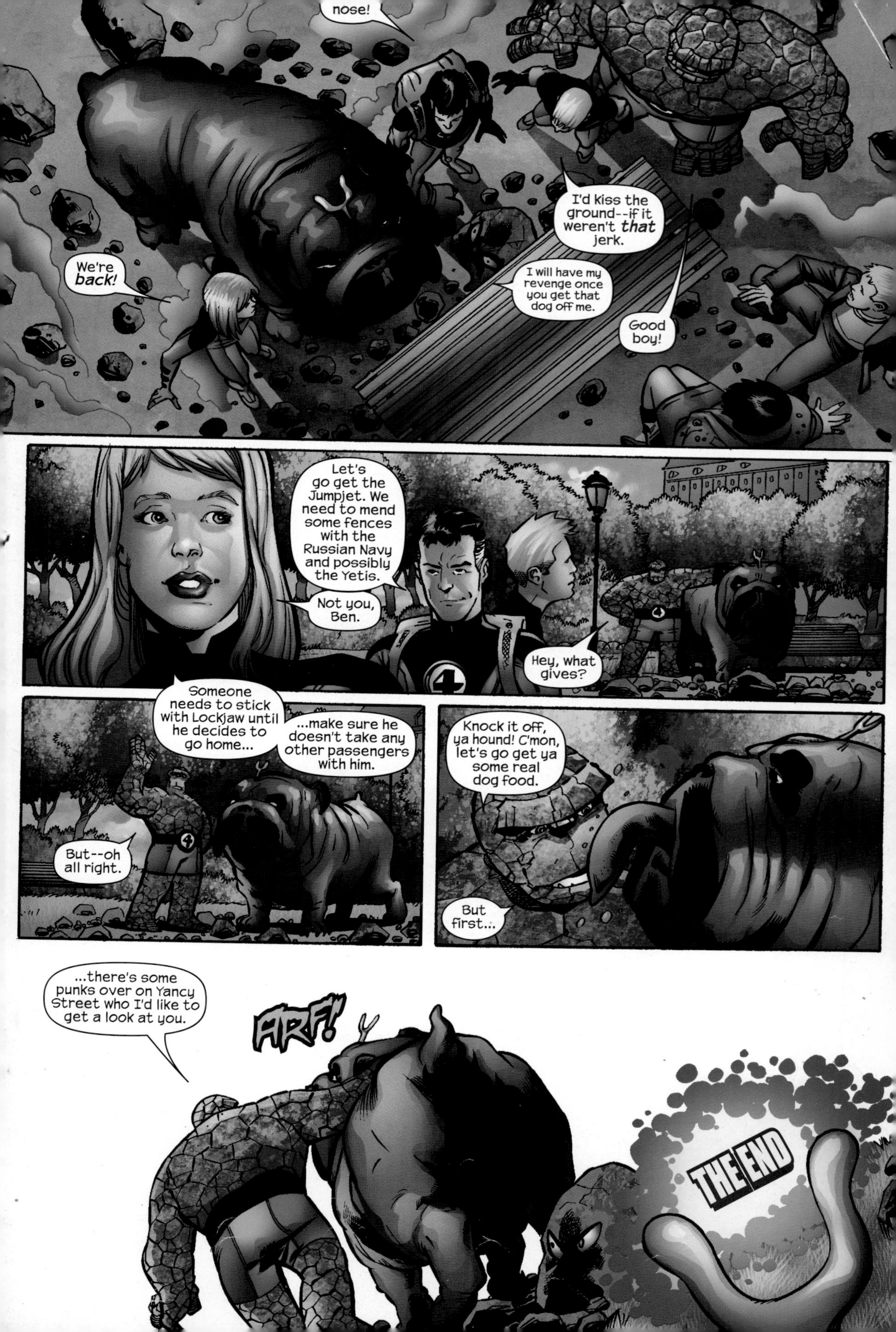
nose!
We're back!
I'd kiss the ground--if it weren't that jerk.
I will have my revenge once you get that dog off me.
Good boy!
Let's go get the Jumpjet. We need to mend some fences with the Russian Navy and possibly the Yetis.
Not you, Ben.
Hey, what gives?
Someone needs to stick with Lockjaw until he decides to go home...
...make sure he doesn't take any other passengers with him.
But--oh all right.
Knock it off, ya hound! C'mon, let's go get ya some real dog food.
But first...
...there's some punks over on Yancy Street who I'd like to get a look at you.
ARF!
THE END

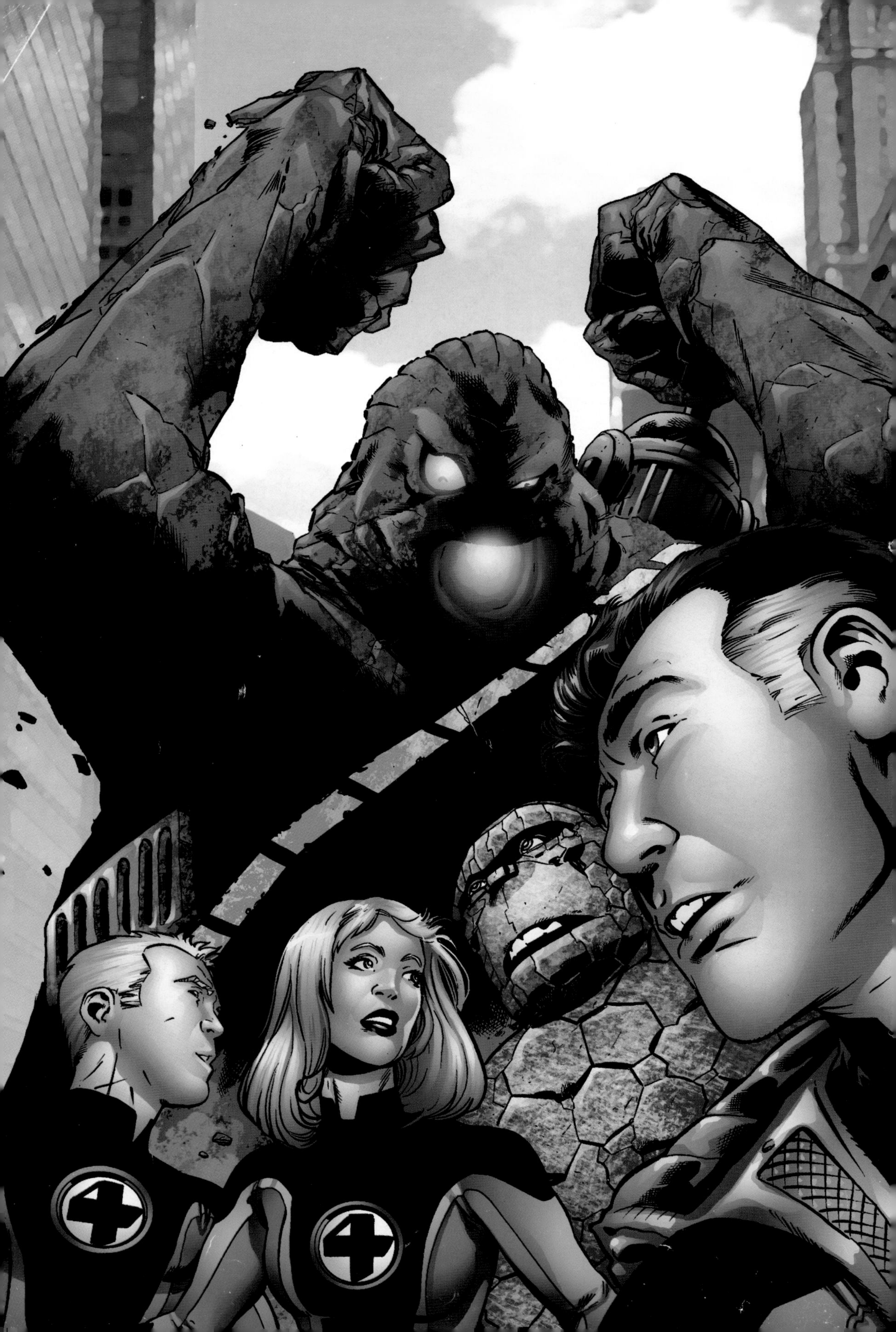